Happy Birthday, ~SpongeBob!

by J-P Chanda
illustrated by Heather Martinez

Ready-to-Read

Simon Spotlight/Nickelodeon

New York   London   Toronto   Sydney

Stephen Hillenburg

Based on the TV series *SpongeBob SquarePants*® created by Stephen Hillenburg
as seen on Nickelodeon®

SIMON SPOTLIGHT
An imprint of Simon & Schuster Children's Publishing Division
1230 Avenue of the Americas, New York, New York 10020

Manufactured in the United States of America

First Edition
2 4 6 8 10 9 7 5 3 1

Library of Congress Cataloging-in-Publication Data
Chanda, J-P.
Happy birthday, SpongeBob! / by J-P Chanda ; illustrated by Heather Martinez.— 1st ed.
p. cm. — (Ready-to-read) "SpongeBob SquarePants."
"Based on the TV series SpongeBob SquarePants created by Stephen Hillenburg as seen on Nickelodeon."
Summary: It is SpongeBob's birthday, but everyone seems to have forgotten.
ISBN 0-689-87674-2
[1. Birthdays—Fiction. 2. Surprise—Fiction. 3. Parties—Fiction. 4. Marine animals—Fiction.] I. Title: Happy birthday,
SpongeBob! II. Martinez, Heather, ill. III. SpongeBob SquarePants (Television program) IV. Title. V. Series.
PZ7.C35927Hap 2005   [E]—dc22   2004016212

It was  birthday!

SPONGEBOB'S

July

"I hope there will be and !" said .

GIFTS   CAKE   SPONGEBOB

"I love and

BALLOONS   PARTY HATS

and !"

KRABBY PATTIES

"Meow?" asked.

GARY

 looked on

SPONGEBOB

as slid by.

GARY

Did forget

my birthday?

wondered SPONGEBOB.

 was pushing

a big .

"Is that a ?"

asked .

"No, it is my new ,"
CHAIR

said .
SANDY

 sat on the .
SANDY   BOX

 did not say
SANDY

"Happy Birthday."

"Do **you** know what day it is?" asked his friend

SPONGEBOB

 . "It starts with

PATRICK

a B...."

"I know! I know!"

said .
PATRICK

" Day! 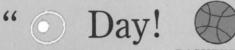 Day!
BUBBLE   BASKETBALL

 Day?"
BUMBLEBEE

 shook his head.
SPONGEBOB

Did everyone forget

the  and ?

GIFTS   CAKE

Did everyone forget
the and
BALLOONS   PARTY HATS
and ?
KRABBY PATTIES
wondered .
SPONGEBOB

went to work.

SPONGEBOB

The was empty!

KRUSTY KRAB

"Hello?"  called out.

SPONGEBOB

SQUIDWARD walked in

and stood next to a TABLE.

"What are you holding?"

asked SPONGEBOB.

"This is my new wig," said  .

SQUIDWARD

SQUIDWARD put the 🧹 on his

MOP

head.

"  , do you know

what day it is?"

asked .

"It is a day to make
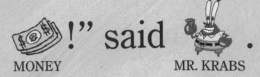!" said 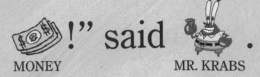.
MONEY   MR. KRABS

"Into the kitchen,

!"
SPONGEBOB

"It looks like everyone forgot my birthday," said .

SPONGEBOB

"No , no , and

GIFTS   CAKE

no for me."

BALLOONS

" !"  called.

SPONGEBOB   MR. KRABS

"Come in here!"

"Surprise!" everyone
yelled.

"Happy Birthday,  !"
SPONGEBOB

It was a big party

with and !

GIFTS   BALLOONS

There were  . . .

PARTY HATS

Happy Birthday, SpongeBob!

. . . and  KRABBY PATTIES

with CANDLES on top!

"You did not forget!"

said SPONGEBOB. "Hooray!"